# ACORN
## WAS A LITTLE
# WILD

Written by JEN ARENA   Illustrated by JESSICA GIBSON

Simon & Schuster Books for Young Readers
New York   London   Toronto   Sydney   New Delhi

# ACORN

was a wild little thing,
pointy on one end and
capped on the other.

He was the first
of his generation to
jump off the tree.

"Don't do that,"
said Oak. "Squirrels
will get you."

"I don't
care about
squirrels,"
said Acorn.
"I just
want to
ROLL."

And roll he did.

He liked the feel of the
sun on his face and the
wind against his cap.

He even took
to taunting the
squirrels.

Nah-
nah - nah - nah-
nah!

Sure enough, just as Oak
had warned, a squirrel got him.
She scooped Acorn into her paws
and scrambled up a tree.

And Acorn loved it, because
Acorn was a wild little thing.
He loved the thrill of the climb
and the kick of bounding
from branch to branch.

Then the squirrel took a nibble of Acorn.

Acorn did NOT love that.

Whoa, whoa, whoa!
Wait a minute there,
buddy!

Before the squirrel could nibble more, a dog
came along. And the dog and the squirrel
barked back and forth until the squirrel
forgot all about Acorn and dropped him.

And the rush, man, the rush of falling from the tree!
It was even better than when Acorn
had jumped that first time from Oak.

Acorn hit the ground and rolled down the hill again.

He sat in the grass for days and days, and the rain came and pounded on his shell like a good Swedish massage, and Acorn loved that, because Acorn was wild that way.

Eventually, another squirrel found Acorn.
"Let's go, go, GO!" Acorn cheered.
"I want to feel the wind against my cap!"

But the squirrel didn't
carry him up a tree.

The squirrel took Acorn
and buried him
deep in the ground.

And that was no fun at all.

But after a while, Acorn noticed cool things going on down there.

The worms were so chill, wiggling around and tickling him as they passed, and Acorn laughed when they did, because even underground, Acorn was still a little wild.

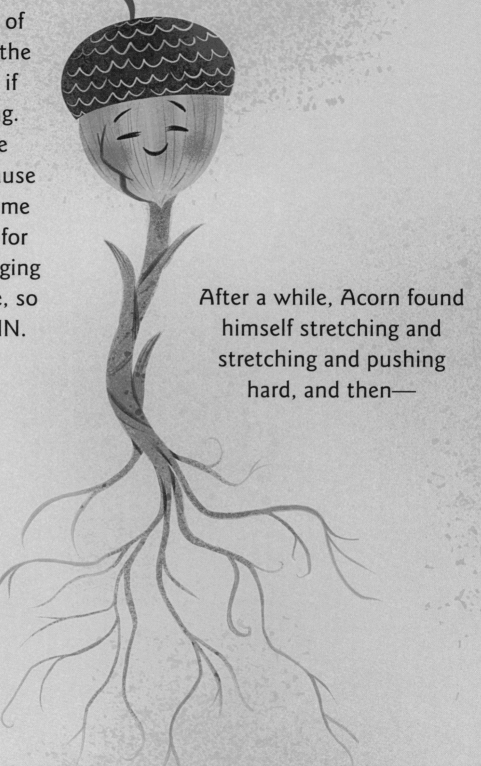

Acorn had a lot of time to think in the dark. He felt as if he was changing. He didn't quite understand, because he'd been the same wild little acorn for so long. But changing was an adventure, so Acorn was ALL IN.

After a while, Acorn found himself stretching and stretching and pushing hard, and then—

He felt the sun for the first time in ages.
Acorn had grown out of his cap and
popped right up through the ground.
And it was SO COOL.

He liked it so much,
he put down a few
more roots and
kept on growing.

Day after day,

week after week,

month after month,

year after year.

Acorn hadn't lost his wild side. Sometimes
he shook his leaves after a summer storm and
rumble-laughed when the squirrels got all wet.

And if a fox peed on his trunk?
He dropped a stick on its noggin.

He never told another acorn,
"Don't do that." He always
said, "Go for it!"

And when the sun was low and the moon was high and the owls hooted in the night, he called all his friends together.

And he loved every minute.
Because Acorn was an oak . . .

but still a little wild inside.

For Katherine and Evelyn.
May you grow into mighty oaks.
—J. A.

For my loving, supportive family.
—J. G.

SIMON & SCHUSTER BOOKS FOR YOUNG READERS
An imprint of Simon & Schuster Children's Publishing Division
1230 Avenue of the Americas, New York, New York 10020
Text © 2022 by Jen Arena • Illustration © 2022 by Jessica Gibson
Book design by Lizzy Bromley © 2022 by Simon & Schuster, Inc.
SIMON & SCHUSTER BOOKS FOR YOUNG READERS and related
marks are trademarks of Simon & Schuster, Inc.
For information about special discounts for bulk purchases, please contact
Simon & Schuster Special Sales at 1-866-506-1949 or business@simonandschuster.com.
The Simon & Schuster Speakers Bureau can bring authors to your live event.
For more information or to book an event, contact the Simon & Schuster Speakers Bureau
at 1-866-248-3049 or visit our website at www.simonspeakers.com.
The text for this book was set in ITC Goudy Sans.
The illustrations for this book were rendered digitally in Photoshop and with a Wacom tablet.
Manufactured in China • 1221 SCP • First Edition
2 4 6 8 10 9 7 5 3 1
Library of Congress Cataloging-in-Publication Data
Names: Arena, Jen, author. | Gibson, Jessica (Illustrator), illustrator.
Title: Acorn was a little wild / Jen Arena ; illustrated by Jessica Gibson.
Description: First edition. | New York : Simon & Schuster Books for Young Readers, [2022] | Audience: Ages 4–8. |
Audience: Grades K–1. | Summary: Acorn is the first one off the tree, longing for adventure and new experiences (though
maybe not being eaten), but when a squirrel buries Acorn he is forced to stay still in the dark
until the exciting changes begin, and he grows into a mighty oak—though at heart he is still a little wild.
Identifiers: LCCN 2021009689 (print) | LCCN 2021009690 (ebook) |
ISBN 9781534483156 (hardcover) | ISBN 9781534483163 (ebook)
Subjects: LCSH: Acorns—Juvenile fiction. | Oak—Juvenile fiction. | Picture books for children. |
CYAC: Acorns—Fiction. | Oak—Fiction. | LCGFT: Picture books.
Classification: LCC PZ7.1.A74 Ac 2022 (print) | LCC PZ7.1.A74 (ebook) | DDC 813.6 [E]—dc23
LC record available at https://lccn.loc.gov/2021009689
LC ebook record available at https://lccn.loc.gov/2021009690